D0374502

MIA MAYHEM #7

GETS X-RAY SPECS

ZZZZZ!

BY **KARA WEST**   ILLUSTRATED BY **LEEZA HERNANDEZ**

LITTLE SIMON

New York London Toronto Sydney New Delhi

LITTLE SIMON

An imprint of Simon & Schuster Children's Publishing Division

1230 Avenue of the Americas, New York, New York 10020

First Little Simon paperback edition April 2020

Copyright © 2020 by Simon & Schuster, Inc.

Also available in a Little Simon hardcover edition

All rights reserved, including the right of reproduction in whole or in part in any form.

LITTLE SIMON is a registered trademark of Simon & Schuster, Inc., and associated colophon is a trademark of Simon & Schuster, Inc.

For information about special discounts for bulk purchases, please contact Simon & Schuster Special Sales at 1-866-506-1949 or business@simonandschuster.com.

The Simon & Schuster Speakers Bureau can bring authors to your live event. For more information or to book an event contact the Simon & Schuster Speakers Bureau at 1-866-248-3049 or visit our website at www.simonspeakers.com.

Designed by Laura Roode

Manufactured in the United States of America 0320 MTN

2 4 6 8 10 9 7 5 3 1

This book has been cataloged with the Library of Congress.

ISBN 978-1-5344-6101-7 (hc)

ISBN 978-1-5344-6100-0 (pbk)

ISBN 978-1-5344-6102-4 (eBook)

CONTENTS

GLASSES?!

Hey there! Can you read what's written on that board?

I have no idea why Ms. Jemison, my teacher, is writing so small.

We're learning about the parts of a flower, and I'd tell you what each part was called . . . if I could actually . . . *see* it.

I squinted my eyes as hard as I could.

But the flower was still blurry, so I inched up some more, until—

OOF!

I slipped out of my chair and fell right on my butt!

My cheeks grew red as my best friend, Eddie Stein, helped me up. Embarrassing things like this happen to me all the time.

I used to think it was because I was a super-klutz. But on one fateful day, I got a special letter telling me that I was actually . . . SUPER!

Like for real!

My name's Mia Macarooney, and *I. Am. A. Superhero!*

And my life hasn't been the same since.

For one thing I now go to *two* schools. In the mornings I go to Normal Elementary School, where I study regular subjects like math and science. Then in the afternoons I head over to a top secret superhero training academy called the Program for In Training Superheroes, aka the PITS. And at the PITS, I go by Mia Mayhem! At *that* school I learn things like how to save somebody from being stuck in a volcano!

Not that there are any volcanoes in my town.

But you get me.

Nobody at my regular school knows my secret identity—except for Eddie, who, at the moment, was staring at

me with a worried look on his face.

"Are you okay, Mia?" he whispered.

I rubbed my eyes and shook my head.

"Is everything all right?" Ms. Jemison asked, looking over at us.

"I can't read the board," I said. "Can you please write bigger?"

"That's odd," my teacher said. "Why don't you come up to the front?"

So I gave it a shot. But it was no use.

Everything was still really hazy, and my head was starting to hurt.

I think Ms. Jemison could tell I wasn't feeling well because she sent me to Mrs. Feelbetter, our school nurse.

9

At the nurse's office, I first got my temperature taken. Nothing seemed out of the ordinary, so Mrs. Feelbetter told me to cover my left eye and read from a letter chart. Then I did the same for the right eye.

I waited quietly as she jotted some notes down.

"Oh, Mia. I think you may need glasses!"

I couldn't believe it. Having to wear glasses was going to change everything, and I was *not* happy about it.

But when I told Eddie the bad news after school, he didn't have the same reaction as me. "Getting glasses isn't really *bad* news. Think of it as getting a pair of cool new shades!" he cried. "To be honest I've always wanted a pair."

He put his hand on my shoulder and gave me a big smile. Eddie always knew how to make me feel better.

And the more I thought about it, a pair of sleek lightning-bolt glasses suddenly didn't sound so bad.

CHAPTER 2

DR. I. SPY

I sped over to the building next door and quick-changed into my supersuit.

On the outside the PITS looked like an old, abandoned warehouse. But on the inside it was the coolest place ever!

I squeezed into an elevator and went up to the second floor, where all the junior-level classes were held.

Inside the gym I looked around for my friends on the bleachers. My vision was still really blurry, but even in the haze, there was no way I could miss the two kids who were excitedly waving their arms.

"Hey, Mia, over here!" cried Penn Powers and Allie Oomph.

When I first met Penn, I thought he was a show-off. But now he's a really good friend. And so is Allie. The three of us met in Dr. Dash's Fast class and became friends in a flash.

"Hey, guys! If you hadn't waved, I would have totally missed you. My vision is really weird today," I said.

"No way—us too! We only knew it was you because of the colors of your suit!" they both cried.

I wanted to ask more questions, but the entire gym suddenly got quiet.

Up at the front, a man had walked in. He was wearing a royal blue supersuit that had large dragonfly wings on each shoulder.

"So nice to—ahem—*see* you all," he said. "My name is Dr. I. Spy. Before we begin our first lesson, tell me: Has anyone been having trouble seeing in class?"

Every single hand shot into the air.

"Ah, well I have good news, young heroes! You're here today to learn how to control your super-sight!"

I glanced over at my friends, but they just shrugged.

"Super-sight usually kicks in at age eight. Things always start off really blurry. But don't worry. You'll soon be able to do awesome things like x-ray through walls and see in absolute darkness!"

Allie and I gave each other a big high five.

"Now, before we use any powers, I'll need each of you to take the PITS eye exam to get fitted for your own pair of super-specs!"

Whoa! Did you hear that?

Sounds like I *do* need glasses after all! Just not the ordinary kind.

Dr. I. Spy pushed a button on his watch, and a fancy steel machine lifted up from the floor.

"Okay, everyone. Who'd like to give this a go?" he asked.

There was a long pause.

Even if it was for x-ray vision, this exam wasn't one I was going to take first.

OOOOOOOH!

I whipped around to see where the
sound had come from.

"Um . . . I'll go," said a voice from all the way in the back. All eyes looked up as a boy in a blazing orange suit came to the front, led by an adorable, furry sidekick.

A New Student

Everyone oohed and aahed as a Labrador retriever wearing a matching supersuit led the way. The kid was also already wearing a sleek pair of shaded rectangular glasses.

"Thanks for volunteering!" Dr. I. Spy exclaimed. The boy nodded. Then the dog barked joyfully, as if he were waiting for something.

"Oh, sorry, of course," said Dr. I. Spy. Then he pushed another button. A much smaller machine, which looked identical to the big one, appeared. The dog stepped up to it and waited.

"Part one is just a simple eye exam," Dr. I. Spy said. "Both of you, please put your faces against your machines. Then look through the lenses and tell me what you see on the other side."

WHIRRRRRR!

From where I sat I could see that there was a large poster in front of the machines. But it was way too blurry for me to make out.

I watched as the boy ran his hand along the top of the lens and felt for where he was supposed to place his chin.

"I don't see anything. It's totally dark," the boy said.

"All right, that's okay," Dr. I. Spy said as he jotted down notes.

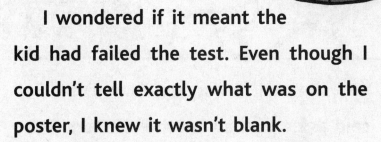

I wondered if it meant the kid had failed the test. Even though I couldn't tell exactly what was on the poster, I knew it wasn't blank.

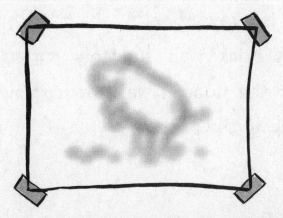

"The real fun starts now," Dr. I. Spy said as he pushed another button. "Part two is x-ray vision!"

A brick wall suddenly sprang up from the floor. It was now completely blocking the poster.

"I'd like for you to focus hard and try to look through the wall. Tell me what you see on the other side," Dr. I. Spy said as he adjusted the lens.

Obviously, if the boy couldn't see the poster the first time, I was sure a wall wasn't going to help—except this time he had an answer!

"I see a poster of a dancing hippo!" the kid cried happily.

His dog yipped in agreement.

"Perfect!" said Dr. I. Spy, smiling. "Great job, both of you!"

Whoa. I totally had not expected that.

I inched closer to try to see how he saw that, but Dr. I. Spy quickly moved on to the next section.

"And now, part three," Dr. I. Spy continued, "is testing your night vision!"

With a snap of his fingers, the lights went out.

SNAP!

It was so dark that I couldn't even see my hand in front of my face! But just like before, the boy instantly had an answer.

"There's an elephant with a hot dog!" he said.

His dog barked a third time.

"Oh yes, that's correct. Great work!" said Dr. I. Spy. Then he snapped his fingers, and the lights came back on. "That's it for now. You can go back to your seat."

How did this kid just go from seeing *nothing* to literally seeing *through a wall?*

I had no idea how he did it, but it sure was impressive.

And it turns out I wasn't the only one who thought so, because the whole class burst into applause.

CHAPTER 4

Mia Takes the Test

After watching this kid and his awesome dog, the test looked much easier than I had first thought, so I raised my hand to go next.

Dr. I. Spy welcomed me down to the floor. Then I put my face up to the lens. But as soon as I did, I felt like I was back in Mrs. Feelbetter's office.

"What do you see?" Dr. I. Spy asked.

The picture on the poster was unclear, so Dr. I. Spy kept switching the lens until I told him to stop.

After ten turns I could finally see it.

"There is a sea lion playing mini golf!" I cried.

"Yes, terrific!" Dr. I. Spy said as he made some notes. "Time for part two!"

He pushed another button, and the same brick wall came up. And just like that the rest of the exam went downhill—fast.

No matter how hard I squinted,
jumped, or spun around, all I saw was
a big ole brick wall.

Dr. I. Spy patted me on the back and
told me to take my time.

So I took
a deep breath
and tried again.

And again.

And again.

By the fifth try I just blurted out
the first thing that came to my mind.

"I think . . . ," I began slowly. "Is it a
singing flower?"

Dr. I. Spy made a quick note. Judging by the look he gave me, that was *not* the right answer. But we still moved on to part three.

He snapped his fingers, and the gym instantly went dark again.

Oh boy. This was even worse than the wall! I could feel beads of sweat dripping down my face.

"Can you tell me what you see?" Dr. I. Spy asked.

I took a deep breath and tried again. But I couldn't see a thing, so I decided to guess. Because that *had* to be better than nothing, right?

"Umm . . . I see a giraffe on roller skates . . . holding a milkshake . . . while riding in a hot-air balloon!"

Oh boy. What was I saying?

I put my hand over my mouth to stop myself from blurting anything else out.

Dr. I. Spy chuckled, recorded more notes, then snapped his fingers.

When the lights came back on, Dr. I. Spy looked at me with a worried frown.

Oh no. Maybe blurting out answers was a bad idea. But it was too late.

Back at my seat I watched as the rest of the class took their tests. Somehow nobody else seemed as panicked as I had been.

When everyone had finished, Dr. I. Spy told us to wait in the student lounge while our glasses were made.

My friends and I were walking out when I heard a familiar snicker.

"Hey, Mia! Nice job using your *loser* vision," Hugo Fast, the class bully, called out.

I glanced over at Allie and Penn, who gave me half-hearted smiles.

The looks on their faces didn't lie. My eyes were *really* bad.

CHAPTER 5

BEN OCULAR AND SEEKER

I walked behind Allie and Penn, lost in my own thoughts.

Before I knew it, we stepped through cool disco lights and into the lounge. I loved it here because it was the perfect hangout spot. There was a quiet area with study pods on one side and an awesome arcade on the other. My friends and I went over to the pinball machine.

That's when I noticed a group of kids behind us, laughing.

When the crowd finally parted, Penn, Allie, and I looked to see who was there. It turned out that everyone wanted to meet the kid with the cool dog!

And we did too. So my friends and I walked over to where he was sitting.

Even with dark shades on, the new kid could tell I was right in front of him.

"Hi. I'm Ben Ocular," he said. Then he waved toward his dog. "And this is Seeker."

Allie, Penn, and I introduced ourselves. Then, just like everyone else, we had a bunch of questions, like how was he already so good at x-ray vision and seeing in the dark?

"I'm terrible at controlling my super-sight. In fact, I think I got everything wrong," I said with a sigh.

"Oh, I wouldn't be so good, either, except that I've been practicing it for a long time."

"What do you mean?" Penn asked.

"Well, I was born blind, so I can't see anything. I need Seeker to help me in regular everyday situations. But the neat thing is that my night vision kicked in much sooner since I was already used to the dark!"

"That's so cool!" the three of us cried.

"X-ray vision is still pretty new for me, too, but now that Seeker and I will have upgraded glasses, we'll be all set."

Seeker quietly sat up straight as Ben scratched his chin.

"So, does Seeker go everywhere with you?" Penn asked.

"Pretty much! My super-senses are much weaker when we aren't together," Ben replied.

"That's why you're a dynamic duo!" cried Penn.

"Pfft, I don't know about that,"
Hugo scoffed. "It's not that impressive
if you already use your super-sight
every day."

Then he stomped away.

"Don't listen to him," I said. "We
saw how great you did."

Ben nodded his head and smiled as Seeker nuzzled against him.

Soon Dr. I. Spy called us back to class with exciting news: Our super-specs were now ready to wear!

CHAPTER
6

A-Mazing

Back in the gym, Dr. I. Spy handed out everyone's glasses. Even Seeker got a pair.

But when he got to me, he paused. "Sorry, Mia. Your prescription is quite strong, so they're a bit . . . chunky."

A *bit* chunky?

Whatever our training exercise was, it was *not* going to be any fun wearing these.

Penn, Allie, and I tried on our glasses.
My friends looked really cool . . . but
not me.

I wished I could take the exam again,
but it was too late. I'd have to make do
with my super-chunky specs.

Soon Dr. I. Spy clapped his hands,
and another hidden door appeared.
Then he quickly led us
down a long spiral
staircase. Dr. I. Spy
entered a secret
code at the door.

BEEP!

439**

BEEP!

When we entered into a vault, a gigantic steel maze was standing in front of us.

"This top secret vault," he said, "is where you'll practice your super-sight skills today! I'll be dividing you into

pairs. One of you will have to find a good hiding spot in the maze. You will have five minutes to hide. Then before the timer beeps, your partner will need to find you by using only x-ray and night vision."

"Cool! It's like super-sight hide-and-seek!" cried Allie.

"That's right!" said Dr. I. Spy. "There's just one catch: None of your non-vision-related powers work down here. The only way to find one another is to focus on your targets and scan *through* the walls."

He split us up, and I ended up being paired with Ben.

"I'll try not to mess it up for us," I said quietly.

"Oh, you'll be fine," Ben said with a smile. "In fact, I'll go into the maze first."

I tried to tell him that was a bad idea, but he had already stepped forward.

A few minutes later Dr. I. Spy sent the first group in to hide. Allie was a seeker, like me, so we watched as Penn, Ben (and Seeker), and Hugo disappeared into the maze.

Five minutes later Dr. I. Spy sent the
rest of us in.

I looked up in awe at the steel walls
that towered over us.

I had no idea how I was going to find Ben, so I did the most obvious thing first: yell out his name at the top of my lungs.

But that didn't help at all. I listened helplessly as my voice echoed down the long halls.

After going in countless circles, I finally stopped and stared hard at the wall.

And then guess what?

Out of nowhere a blast of heat lasers came out of my eyes! In just one shot I burned through five walls, creating a tunnel that went straight through the center of the maze!

And I had no idea what I did or how I did it.

I stepped onto the path I created,
not sure where it would lead.

But as soon as I did, the whole maze
was plunged into darkness.

THE MISSING POOCH

Even though it was dark, I found exactly who I was looking for at the end of the path.

"Hey, Ben! I am so glad I found you—" I started to say. But as soon as I looked closer, I knew something was wrong.

"Oh, Mia! I'm so glad you're here!" he cried. "I was in trouble here by myself."

"So glad you're okay," I said calmly.
"Tell me exactly what happened."

Ben straightened up as he took a
big breath.

"Everything was fine until about two minutes in. A gust of wind bulldozed past me without any warning! I fell over, and when I got up, Seeker was gone!"

I could tell how worried Ben was.

"He never leaves me. This doesn't make sense!" he cried. "And to make matters worse, my glasses are shattered!"

He handed them to me, and sure enough, they were broken into several pieces.

"Without my dog *or* my glasses, I'm going to need your help, Mia," Ben said.

"Okay. You got it," I said. I knew that together we'd find a way out of this giant puzzle.

I put Ben's hand on my arm. In Seeker's absence I would need to become Ben's eyes. I didn't know which way to go, but I knew we should get moving. Slowly, I made left and right turns at each corner. But after a while we were still totally lost.

Luckily that's when Ben stepped in with an idea.

"My x-ray vision may not work without my glasses. But my super-sight is strong enough to sense the walls around us!" he said. "Come on. Let's go this way!"

I followed as Ben led the way by feeling for specific vibrations along the walls. We knew that all sounds echoed and bounced off one another in this maze. And it turned out that there was a very special perk to having a superdog sidekick: Ben and Seeker both had the ability to sense each other's locations.

"It's kind of like having a mental GPS connection!" Ben explained.

"That's so cool!" I exclaimed.

Just as we were about to make a left, Ben turned back around. "Hey, someone is up ahead."

After squinting as hard as I could, two images came into focus.

"Hello?" I said. "Who's there?"

"Mia, is that you?" asked a familiar voice.

I broke into a huge smile. I would recognize that voice anywhere.

HEAT LASER TIME!

"Allie and Penn! I'm so glad you're here. We need your help!" I cried frantically.

Ben and I filled them in on the situation, and then we came up with a game plan.

"Since Seeker never leaves me," Ben concluded, "something must really be wrong."

"Of course we'll help!" said Allie.

"We've got to get the dynamic duo back together!"

But with the four of us, it was hard trying to not walk into walls.

Penn banged his elbow and groaned. "It sure would be so much easier if we could use our other powers," he said. "Like fly up over the maze to find the exit."

"Yeah," said Allie. "Or run fast all the way through it."

That's when I remembered: There had been so much going on that I'd forgotten about what I had done by mistake earlier. "Umm, so I did use another power, actually."

"What?!" Penn and Allie exclaimed.

"I didn't mean to," I said quickly. "It just happened. I was concentrating really hard, trying to tap into my x-ray vision. And instead of doing any scanning, my eyes blasted heat lasers and burned a hole into several walls!"

"No way!" said Ben. "So this means I was right!"

"About what?" I asked.

"You *are* great at super-sight! Heat laser beams isn't a *different* power—it's a type of super-sight! Just a really advanced and harder type!"

"Wow, you've got heat lasers?" Penn asked. "That's *awesome*!"

"Yeah, but guess what's even more awesome?" asked Allie. "Heat lasers don't just blast through things. They fix things too!"

"What? They fix things?" I asked.

"Like . . . broken glasses?" asked Penn.

Ben gasped. "Will you try to fix my glasses?"

I bit my lip while I tried to decide. On one hand, I definitely wanted to help my friend. On the other hand, I had *no idea* how to control my heat lasers. What if I melted the glasses instead?

"Please, Mia?" said Ben.

"Oh, all right," I said with a sigh. "Just . . . if I melt them, please don't get mad."

"Of course!" said Ben. "But trust me. I have a good feeling about this."

"Me too," said Allie.

"Me three," said Penn.

I took Ben's broken glasses and placed them on the floor. Then I had everyone stand back.

Just like before, I focused really hard.

But nothing happened.

So I just stared.

And stared.

And stared.

All of a sudden it worked! Heat lasers beamed out of my eyes and landed right on Ben's glasses. I held my gaze straight until I finally had to blink.

As I rubbed my eyes, Allie picked up
the glasses.

"Are they melted?" I asked, my voice
a bit shaky.

Allie carefully looked at them from every angle and then gave me a big thumbs-up.

It had totally worked!

And with Ben's glasses fixed, we were officially back in business!

CHAPTER 9

THE DYNAMIC DUO REUNITED!

Now that he had his glasses back intact, Ben led the way through the maze. Even without Seeker, his night vision was the strongest.

"I think he's this way," Ben told us as he turned left down a path in the maze.

"How can you tell?" asked Allie. "Can you see him? I still can't see anything."

"I can't see him yet," Ben replied. "But I'm starting to feel vibrations in the wall."

"You can do that, too?" asked Penn.

"Yep!" Ben said. Then he told my friends what he had explained to me earlier. "I may not have regular vision like you, but I'm sensitive to echoes— and I'm getting some very dog-like vibrations from this direction!"

I put my hand against the steel wall, to see if I could feel the dog-like vibrations too. All I felt was cool metal. But that was okay because I just learned I can shoot heat laser beams!

As we walked farther into the maze, I was finally able to ˙see in front of me. Now, I'm not sure if my eyes were adjusting to the dark or if it was that my super-sight was getting stronger.

Either way I was starting to think that having super-sight was really cool after all!

"Okay, guys," Ben said. "We're almost there."

As we got closer to where we thought Seeker was, Ben was walking faster, without even using my arm! I couldn't blame him. If I was part of a dynamic duo, I wouldn't want to be separated either!

Soon we heard a familiar sound.

Seeker's bark echoed off the walls
and filled the entire hallway.

We made two more right turns as we chased the sound of Seeker's voice. Then, on the last turn, we finally found him! Seeker came running toward Ben and happily wagged his tail.

"Hey, boy! What happened? Where'd you go?" Ben asked as he scratched Seeker behind the ears.

So Seeker walked away to show us.

Sitting on the floor not far away was Hugo. And he did *not* look happy.

His hair was a mess, his suit was covered in dirt marks, and he had a red rash all over his face.

Whatever happened between them, it was clear that Hugo and Seeker did *not* get along.

MIA MAYHEM IS SPEC-TACULAR

"Oh, phew!" exclaimed Dr. I. Spy when we finally came out. "I was afraid we were going to have to send in a search party!"

When Dr. I. Spy asked us what happened, we all looked at Hugo and Seeker for answers. Hugo blamed Seeker, and Seeker, well, was clearly just happy to be back with Ben.

It was important to get the facts, and luckily, there were high-tech cameras in the maze.

And here's what had happened:

It turned out that Hugo was the one who broke Ben's glasses. But Hugo explained that was an accident. The reason why he rushed past them was *not* to knock Ben down on purpose. It was actually to get away from Seeker! Because believe it or not, he was allergic to dogs.

Dr. I. Spy knew exactly what to do and gave him special eye drops to make the itchiness go away.

Then, before dismissing class, he called me over too.

"Mia, the cameras showed you using heat lasers inside the maze," he said.

I held my breath, expecting to get into trouble.

But rather than being mad, he gave me a big high five.

He assured me that controlling heat lasers is a hard super-sight skill that will take time to perfect. But for now, one thing was for sure: The fact that I had tapped into heat vision was proof that

I did *not* need those chunky glasses.

Funny, huh?

I guess I should have never guessed during the eye exam and pretended to know something when I didn't. If I hadn't made up those crazy answers,

I probably would have had a much smoother time in the maze.

But on the flip side, if there's anything this adventure has taught me, it's that sometimes it's worth it to learn things the hard way.

After all, thanks to the most chaotic hide-and-seek mission ever, I've learned I have heat vision, helped two best friends reunite, and made an awesome new friend with the coolest superhero sidekick!

I'm going to be a star!

Okay, maybe not *immediately*. First I'm going to ace this audition. *Then* I'm going to be a star.

I'm in my theater class, and I can't wait to get up onstage!

I've been preparing for this moment

Excerpt from *Mia Mayhem Steals the Show!*

ever since Ms. Montgomery, our theater teacher, announced the school play. This year's show is called *How to Be a Good Superhero*.

And guess who happens to be one in real life?

Believe it or not . . . *me*!

Like for real!

My name is Mia Macarooney, and *I. Am. A. Superhero!*

Now, I know I don't look very super right now. When I'm at Normal Elementary School, I'm just a regular kid.

But after this audition is over, I'm going to *another* school called the

Program for In Training Superheroes, aka the PITS! And at *that* place, I go by my superhero name—Mia Mayhem! I've learned how to use all kinds of awesome powers. But really, the most important part of my training has been learning how to be a good superhero.

So that's why I know I'm perfect for this play!

Excerpt from *Mia Mayhem Steals the Show!*